BRENT LIBRARIES

Please return/renew this item
by the last date shown.
Books may also be renewed by
phone or online.
Tel: 0333 370 4700
On-line www.brent.gov.uk/libraryservice

FAMILY DAYS OUT

The Bike Ride

Meet the family

Mum

Amma

Milly

Ben

FAMILY DAYS OUT

Jackie Walter and Jem Maybank

The Bike Ride

W

FRANKLIN WATTS

LONDON • SYDNEY

"Let's go on a bike ride," said Mum.

"We could go to the woods," said Amma.

"Yes!" cried Ben.

"Boring," moaned Milly.

Mum and Amma packed up a picnic.

Ben found their helmets.

Milly was busy on her phone.

"Come on, Milly, we're ready!" said Mum.

"Only if I can bring my phone," said Milly.

"If you must," smiled Mum.

It was cool in the woods beneath the trees.
The leaves fluttered in the breeze.
The sunlight sparkled on the stream.

"What a lovely day!" said Amma.
But Milly was having a problem.
"I can't get any signal!" she muttered.

9

"Let's have a race!" said Ben.
"First one to the gate wins!"
Mum and Amma laughed.
"You're on," said Amma. "Come on,
Milly, bet you can't beat us!"

But Milly was still trying to make her phone work. The others raced off.

"This phone is rubbish!" Milly complained.
She sped off to catch up with the others.

But Ben had already won.

"Not fair! You didn't wait for me to start," said Milly.

"New race! First one to the stream wins!" said Amma.

"On your marks, get set, GO!" shouted Mum.

15

All four of them raced down the muddy hill.
"Not too fast!" shouted Amma.

But Mum didn't brake in time. SPLASH!
She fell into the stream ...
and so did most of the picnic!

Ben and Milly started to laugh.

"Well, we might as well eat what's left of our picnic here," laughed Mum. "That will give you a chance to dry out, too," smiled Amma.

The family sat down and ate the picnic.
Milly tried to make her phone work,
but she did not have a signal.

So Ben and Milly made
a dam across the stream.

They looked for animal
homes along the bank.

"I'm still hungry," complained Ben.

"Me too!" said Milly.

"I think I owe you all a treat
at the café, don't I?" Mum smiled.

"YES!" shouted Ben. "Race you there?"
"Very funny, Ben, I think we'll take it
a bit slower this time," laughed Amma.

At the café, they all ordered hot chocolate
and slices of cake.

FREE WI-FI

Mum pointed to a sign. "Look, Milly, they have Wi-Fi – do you want to ask for the password so you can use your phone?"

"It's alright," smiled Milly between mouthfuls. "It can wait."

28

29

A note about sharing this book

The Family Days Out series has been developed to provide a starting point for discussion about families and how these can be made up in many different ways. The series also gives children the chance to reflect on their own family life.

Each book emphasises the importance of spending time together, and shows how family members can support and help each other. The series encourages young children to learn to respect people's differences and treat all kinds of family fairly and without discrimination.

The Bike Ride features a family of two mums, a teenage daughter and a young son. In the story, Milly, the teenage daughter, is reluctant to join in with the family bike ride and would prefer to spend time on her phone. But when she cannot get any signal, she ends up having a great time with her brother Ben and her mums.

HOW TO USE THE BOOK
The book is designed for adults to share with either an individual child, or a group of children.

BEFORE READING THE STORY
Choose a time to read when you and the children are relaxed and have time to share the story without distractions or needing to rush.

Spend time looking at the illustrations and talk about what the book may be about before reading it together.

After reading, talk about the book with the children:

- What was it about? Have the children ever not wanted to go on a family day out? What happened? Did they end up having fun in the end?

- Ask, who are the people in their own family? This might include grandparents or other people who take care of them.

- Ask, who do you help in your family? Who can you ask for help if you need to?

- Discuss what things their family likes doing together. Ask whether all the people in their family like doing the same things, or whether they prefer to do different things? Ask whether there are things they do not like doing with their family? This could perhaps be rowing with a sibling, helping at home or grocery shopping.

- Discuss how their family makes these differences fair for everyone so that they all have a chance to do the things they like, and help with the jobs they dislike.

- To encourage discussion, and help children who find it difficult to join in, you could play a quick-fire game of "Two Good, Two Bad".

ASK:
- What are the two best things you do in your family?
- What are the two worst things you do in your family?

You could note their answers down in a tally chart and use the results to make a bar graph about top family likes and dislikes.

First published in Great Britain in 2018
by The Watts Publishing Group

Copyright © The Watts Publishing Group 2018

Series Editor: Sarah Peutrill
Series Designer: Peter Scoulding

A CIP catalogue record for this book is
available from the British Library.

ISBN 978 1 4451 5880 8

Printed in China

MIX
Paper from
responsible sources
FSC® C104740

Franklin Watts
An imprint of
Hachette Children's Group
Part of The Watts Publishing Group
Carmelite House
50 Victoria Embankment
London EC4Y 0DZ

An Hachette UK Company
www.hachette.co.uk

www.franklinwatts.co.uk